Bite this Book
the book you read to your dog

Written by Lony Ruhmann

Cover by Lisa Siegel
Illustrated by Pritali Joharapurkar

To Juve, my love

ISBN 978-1-61225-188-2

Published by Mirror Publishing
Milwaukee, WI 53214

Printed in the USA.

INTRODUCTION

When Juve, my very first dog, was a puppy, he came down with a terrible disease called distemper. The effects of the disease were harsh. He could not stand up on his own; He could not go to the bathroom on his own; He had to be fed via a baby bottle. He was always in his bed and almost always hot.

In his bed, he would oftentimes look at me with his big eyes and make different sounds. I started to listen to what he had to say. With the help of a close friend, who also happened to be an animal communicator, I learned that a lot of his utterances expressed these sentiments and concerns: "I don't feel good. I am scared. Help me. Love me. I am so worried. Don't give up on me. Touch me." His vulnerability was heart wrenching.

I started to respond back to Juve, in order to reassure him. I told him, "I want you to live. I love you so much. You are a good boy." Based on the name of one of his health supplements, I created a song for him which he adored:

Juve is my sweet, sweet boy,
Juve is my cod liver boy.

Seventy-five percent of puppies diagnosed with distemper do not survive. Juve did.

As I embarked on writing a book specifically to be read to dogs, Juve kept interjecting. He wanted to tell his fellow dogs that he is happy, that he is strong, that he is playful and full of zest. He wanted to be the author. So the following vignettes are primarily his stories, primarily his words, about his life, his love of life.

As I was finishing the book, Juve's pals, Zoey, Maggie, Teddy, Sophie and Rocky also chimed in and presented their passionate tales. This is a book of joy, from Juve and his gang, to be shared with the dog you love.

HAPPY WALK (by Juve)

Happy Walk.
Many smells.
Let me smell.
No hurry,
I take a loooong time to smell.

I like the flower smell,
The tree and grass smell.
Most of all,
I love the doggie,
Pee pee smell.

I love to pee pee many many times.
The best smell of all smells
Is MY pee pee smell.
I am the boss.
My pee pee is everywhere.

I meet another dog in park.
I like dog and say,
Let's be friends.
Let's sniff each other.
Sit down on the grass with me.
I want to look at the other dogs with you.

I say good-bye to dog and we walk some more.
My body relaxes.
It's time to take a big, big poop.
Ah, feel so much better.
You praise my big poop.
I run with joy.

We go home now.
I love my loooong walk.
You talk to me.
You sound sweet. You sound happy.
I am happy too.
I love to walk with you.

PAW UNDERNEATH DOOR (by Juve)

Hey, can't you see me?
Can't you see my paw
Under the door?
I want in.
Let me in.

I am not going to let you
Ignore me.
You can not
Ignore me.
When you look
At the door
You will see only me.
You will not be able
To think of anything
But me.
Now let me in.
Hurry up and
Let me in.

Don't you know
I can wait
This one out?
I will wait this out
And I will win.

Look at my paw.
You will open the door
And let me in.

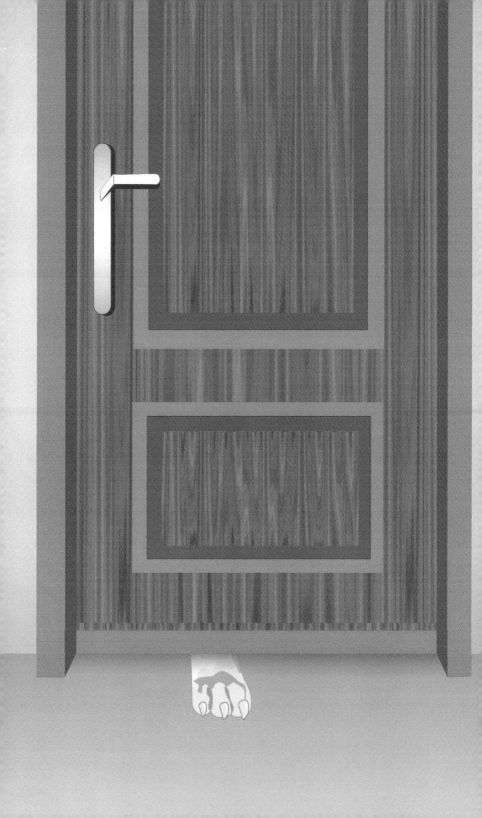

ALONE TIME (by Zoey)

I lay down in your office.
You close the door.
I like that.
No one can come in,
It's just me
With you.

You come down to cuddle.
That's just what I wanted.
I know that this is
A special time,
Alone time.

You rub my neck,
I relax.
You get closer,
I curl up.
You talk softly,
Speaking words of love,
I sigh.
You touch my face,
I kiss your hand.
You rub my tummy,
I snuggle closer.

Inside of me
It feels very quiet,
Very still,
Very sweet,
Very soft.
I know that
I am loved.

THE SQUIRREL (by Teddy)

I Hear an Intruder,
Bark, Bark, Bark.
My Job is to Find the Intruder.
Where are You?
Ha, Ha, I see You!
Bark, Bark, Bark.
Got to get Closer.
Good, You are Close Now.
My Job is to Get You.
Do You Hear Me?
Bark, Bark, Bark.
You Run,
Or I Will Nab You.

SQUEAKY TOY (by Juve)

It's so much fun,
It's so much joy,
My squeaky, squeaky, squeaky toy.

I talk to you
When I squeak my toy.
I tell you
I'm a happy boy.

So hear me now.
I squeak for you.
I tell you that:
I
Love
You.

Squeak
Squeak
Squeak.

I AM FREE (by Juve when he was sick with distemper)

My bones hurt me,
But in my head
I can see myself running,
And I am free.

I am free
To run across big fields
And never stop.

I am free to run faster
Than any person,
Any dog,
Any critter,
Anything.

My body is free.
No aches.
No pain.
Free.

I am Juve.
I am running.
I am free.

FOOD (by Juve)

I like when you cook me food.
I like warm food.
I like warm carrots
and warm rice.
Most of all, I like warm meat.

I smell meat.
What a good smell meat.
It's hard to sit and wait.
Fill my bowl now,
with meat and crunchy skin.

After food, I go to your room
And roll on the carpet.
My tummy feels good.
I bark and bark.
I say, good food.
I say, I feel good.

I bark some more
You love me, I say.
You make me good food.
You make me warm meat.
Woof! Woof! Woof!
Meat! Meat! Meat!

MY DADDY'S FRIENDS (by Juve)

I like when my Daddy's friends
Come to the house,
So I can talk to them.
I tell them,
"I am Juve.
Let me smell your hands.
Touch me.
I want to be friends too.
Hey, look at me!"

GET THE TREAT AND RUN (by Juve)

Happy, Happy, Happy,
Treat, Treat, Treat.
I Love Treats.
I Got it – Good!
I've Got to Run Fast.
Running Fast.
Okay, I'm Safe.
No One Better Come Close.
It's My Treat.
Yum, Treat Yum.
Treat is Mine, Mine, Mine.

THIS YARD IS MINE (by Teddy)

This Yard is Mine,
From the grass on the ground
To the trees in the sky.
Everything
Plants
Bushes
Doors
Chairs
Rocks
Everything is Mine.
Mine, Mine, Mine.

If you make
A scratch
A sound
A step
A peep
A howl
A groan
A blink
A whisper
A groan
A tweek
I will know it.

I am listening.
I am smelling.
I am watching.
I am waiting.

I tell you now
This yard I mine.
Make a move.
Just try.
Please try.
I am waiting for you.

NOT A BATH! (by Juve)

It's a bath, got to run.
Where can I hide?
Where can I be safe?
I do not want to hear my name.
Nobody say my name.
"Juve, bathtime."

Got to think fast.
I'll hide behind his big chair
and be real quiet.
"Juve, I see you, come on let's go."
I'll pretend I did not hear that.
They are getting closer.
This is not good.

They are carrying me to the bath.
The water is getting louder and louder.
They are talking sweetly to me.
But I don't hear the sweet words,
I hear the water.

They are trying to get me to jump
into the tub.
I'll act like my body does not work.
Maybe they'll get tired of this.
Maybe they will give up
and let me go.

They are placing me in the tub now, oh no.
Feel the water on my feet. don't like that.
Why am I in a waterhouse?
Water in pond – good.
In river – good.
Water in house bad!!!

I'll keep to the edge of the bath.
I'll just poke my nose
out the shower door here…

Hey, they are pouring water over me.
What is going on here?
They treat me like a baby,
Don't they know who I am?

Water is everywhere.
Water is all over the place.
They got me now,
I'm all wet.
Got to relax,
I know they got me now.

RUNNING (by Zoey)

I'm running,
I'm running fast.
I love to run.
It's so much fun.
I love my body.
Look at me
I am free.
Nobody catches me.

I want to run.
Please let this last.
Look, I'm so fast.
Just let me run.
I'm not done.
So let me run.
I want to run.

I'm running now.
Look, I'm running now.
I'm running now.
Hee, hee, hee, hee, hee (a happy laugh).

SPOOKY PLACE (by Juve)

Take me to the spooky place
That is very, very dark.
Take me to the spooky place
The real scary park.

I'll be scared of nothing
No critters, hills or trees.
I will find the way home,
Just you wait and see.

Take me to the spooky place,
So scarey and so grave.
Take me to the spooky place,
I'll show you I am brave.

I LIKE IT WHEN YOU TALK TO ME (by Juve)

I hear your voice.
You are talking to me.
I like that.
When you talk to me
I know you want me
to be happy.

I like it when you praise me.
You tell me I am big and strong,
Smart and beautiful.
I know I am loved
And belong here with you.

Sometimes you tell me stories,
like remember when you were a puppy
and we brought you home?
You ran all through the house.
We loved you from the moment we saw you.
We have loved you forever.

I like stories about walks too.
Like remember when we took a walk in the woods
and there was a spooky place?
It was dark and scary.
You took us through the spooky space.
You are such a brave boy.

When you talk to me,
I know most of the words.
The best word is: Good.
Then: Meat and Treat.
Then: Walk.

THE LADY WRESTLER (by Sophie)

I like to wrestle,
I'll knock you down.
I like to wrestle
And roll around.

I like to wrestle
And be on top.
I like to wrestle
And never stop.

I like to wrestle,
I'm a wild, wild girl.
I like to wrestle,
I am going to get you, Grrrrr.

I like to wrestle,
From my head to my toes.
I like to wrestle
And feel you close.

I like to wrestle,
See what I can do!
I like to wrestle
Cause I love you.

FUNNY FACE (by Rocky)

Look at Me Walk
With my Leash
In my Mouth.
Just look at me.

Look at me Fall
Real slow
To the ground.
Do you see me smiling?

Look at my Funny Face.
Talk to me,
Tell me
I am a Funny Boy.

Listen to me.
Listen to my silly sounds.
They will make you laugh.

I want to share
My fun with you,
My love,
And silly joy.

THREE DOGS ON A COUCH
(After their evening walk by Zoey, Juve and Teddy)

We're three dogs on a couch,
Happy
Quiet
Relaxed
Peaceful
Full
Tired
Loved
Grateful
Friends.

SOMETIMES I JUST HAVE TO KISS YOU (by Juve)

Sometimes,
I just have to kiss you.
Your face is close to mine
And I forget about everything
And I kiss
And kiss
And kiss you.

I have a
Big, big
Love for you.
Inside,
You make me twinkle
And sometimes,
I just have to kiss you.

YOU CAN'T CATCH ME! (by Zoey)

You can't catch me
No you can't
I'm too fast for you.

Just when you think
You're getting close
I'll trick you
With my moves.
I'll dodge and dart,
I'll swirl and curl,
I'm such a clever girl

Try to catch me
Ha, ha, ha
I love it when you try
I'll jump and spin
I'll lunge and loop
I'm faster than a fly.

I'm the fastest one,
I'm the fastest girl,
I'm the fastest dog alive.

MOMMY AND DADDY (by Maggie)

Mommy and Daddy came
With a big dog and took me
To my new home.

I was scared the whole day,
And could not eat,
And could not potty.
But Mommy kept holding me.

In the night,
I slept close to her face.
It made me feel warm.

The next day I ate my food
And did my potty.
I hope they will love me.
I think they will love me.

.

FAMILY TRIP (by Juve)

WOWEEE!
Dad just told me
we are going on a family trip.
Dad, Mom, Zoey, and me,
we are all going together.
YIPPEE!

I feel good.
I know I am coming,
I know there will be lots of walks
and lots of special time for me.
Most of all,
we will all be together.

I like it when
we all get in the car
and take the long car ride.
My favorite part is lying between
Mom and Dad in the front seat
with my head on my Daddy's leg.

I know we are going
to a special place.
We are going to the woods.
The woods have many smells,
Spooky places and surprises.

One time I crossed a river
and found a magic place in the woods
where loud water hit big rocks.
This was my big happy.
I felt like such a big boy.
I told you, "I am big like you.
I am the biggest boy ever."

One time I saw a cow lying in his field.
He got up and ran to me
With a big smiley face
and said hello.
I let him smell me.
He tried to lick me, but I moved away.
What a big tongue he had!

At the end of the day, I am tired and sleepy.
I feel peace.
I love us together.
I love the woods.
I know my life is good.
I listen to the sounds of the night and rest with you.

RAIN (by Juve)

Daddy opens the door.
He tells me, "Go bathroom".
I look out at the rain
I can't move,
There's water everywhere.
You expect me to go out in that?
No way!
I go back inside.

After dinner, I have to poop bad.
I go with Daddy outside in the rain.
I try to miss all the big waters.
But I still get wet, too wet.

After I poop,
I run straight home and don't stop.
Get me out of here!
Get me out of this water mess!!!
Daddy laughs at me.
When we get home,
He rubs me nice with a towel.
He makes me warm.

DOGS ARE GOOD (by Juve)

Daddy, I Want to Tell You
Dogs are Good.
In our Deepest Place,
We Love.
In our Deepest Place,
The Love is Sooo Big.

My Love for You is
Bigger than Me,
Bigger than the Park,
Bigger than Everything
I See and Smell.

In My Heart,
I Live to
Love You,
Love Mommy
And Love
All the Animals.

BEDTIME (by Juve)

You lift me up onto your bed.
I walk over to the big pillow:
Swish-kaboom.
I fall into it
And quickly look at you.

I see you smile.
I tell you,
This is my pillow.
This is my special bed.
I know,
this is our special time.

You get in bed too.
You look at me.
You touch me.
You talk to me.
You tell me you love me.

You ask if I remember all the good things
we did today.
The walk, the tug of war, the belly rubs.
I start to remember.
I close my eyes and smile.

Soon I am no longer here.
I am dreaming.
I am with a pack of dogs.
They are my dear friends.
We are running fast.
Everywhere it is beautiful.

In the bed, I move my body closer to yours
and place my front paw over your leg...
and we sleep.

CPSIA information can be obtained
at www.ICGtesting.com
Printed in the USA
LVIW02n0910311013
359380LV00001B/1

* 9 7 8 1 6 1 2 2 5 1 8 8 2 *